Between Earth & Sky

LEGENDS OF NATIVE AMERICAN SACRED PLACES

WRITTEN BY

Joseph Bruchac

ILLUSTRATED BY

Thomas Locker

Harcourt Brace & Company

SAN DIEGO   NEW YORK   LONDON

Requests for permission to make copies of any part of the work should be mailed to: Permissions
Department, Harcourt Brace & Company, 6277 Sea Harbor Drive, Orlando, Florida 32887-6777.

Library of Congress Cataloging-in-Publication Data
Bruchac, Joseph, 1942–
Between earth & sky: legends of Native American sacred places/by Joseph Bruchac; illustrated by
Thomas Locker.—1st ed. p. cm.
Summary: Through the guidance of his uncle and the retelling of various Native American legends,
a young boy learns that everything living and inanimate has its place, should be considered sacred
and given respect.
ISBN 0-15-200042-9
1. Indians of North America—Folklore. 2. Folklore—North America—Juvenile literature.
[1. Indians of North America—Folklore. 2. Folklore—North America.]
I. Locker, Thomas, 1937–   ill. II. Title
E98.F6B8917   1996   [398.2'08997]—dc20   95-10862

First edition
A B C D E

PRINTED IN SINGAPORE

Suggested further reading:

Bahr, Donald, Juan Smith, William Smith Allison, and Julian Hayden. *The Short Swift Time of Gods
on Earth*. Berkeley: University of California Press, 1994.

Mooney, James. *History, Myths and Sacred Formulas of the Cherokee*. Report no. 19. Washington:
Bureau of American Ethnology, 1900.

Parker, Arthur C. *Seneca Myths and Folk Tales*. Buffalo, N. Y.: Buffalo Historical Society, 1923.

Peters, Russell. *The Wampanoag of Mashpee*. n.p., 1987.

Zolbrod, Paul. *Dine Bahane, the Navajo Creation Story*. Albuquerque: University of New Mexico
Press, 1984.

The illustrations in this book were done in oils on canvas.
The display type was hand lettered by Georgia Deaver.
The text type was set in Truesdale.
Map by Anita Karl and James Kemp
Color separations by Bright Arts, Ltd., Singapore
Printed and bound by Tien Wah Press, Singapore
This book was printed with soya-based inks on Leykam recycled
paper, which contains more than 20 percent postconsumer waste
and has a total recycled content of at least 50 percent.
Production supervision by Warren Wallerstein and David Hough
Designed by Michael Farmer

*for my sons,
Jim and Jesse,
whose hearts hold the Seventh Direction*
—J. B.

for my son Joshua
—T. L.

ABOUT THIS BOOK

MANY YEARS AGO, Black Elk, a famous Lakota medicine man, was talking to a writer named John Neihardt about sacred places. Harney Peak in the Black Hills of South Dakota, said Black Elk, is the center of the world. Then, after thinking a moment, Black Elk added, "But anywhere is the center of the world."

The landscape of North America is filled with places that hold deep, sacred meaning to the native people. Some are locations where special ceremonies took place. Other places are related to stories from long ago. Many of those sacred places are connected to lessons that we all need to hear.

Western culture speaks of four directions. Native American cultures throughout the continent recognize seven. There are the cardinal directions of East, South, West, and North, directions that correspond to our life cycle of birth, youth, adulthood, and the time of being an elder, respectively. Then there are the directions of Earth and Sky. These Six Directions are easy to locate. The Seventh Direction, however, is harder to see. It is the direction within us all, the place that helps us see right and wrong and maintain the balance by choosing to live in a good way.

Between Earth & Sky is a book about some of the special places that are sacred to native people. It is also about learning *where* and *how* to look. When we learn this, we will not miss seeing the beauty that is around us and within us as we walk between Earth and Sky.

*L*ITTLE TURTLE and his uncle Old Bear were walking. Little Turtle knew his uncle had many things to teach him.

"This water is another of the gifts from Kit-se-le-mu-kong, our Creator. It cleans our bodies and our minds and sets our spirits on the right path to do things the way they should be done."

Little Turtle understood why his uncle had brought him here. They had come a long way to visit Ma-hi-ka-ni-tewk, the Hudson River land where his Delaware ancestors had lived.

Long ago, those ancestors had to leave this place, but he remembered his grandmother saying to him more than once, "Our bodies left, but our hearts will always live here. It is a sacred place for us."

"Uncle," Little Turtle said, "what is a sacred place? Is this the only sacred place?"

OLD BEAR stopped and knelt, and traced a circle on the soft Earth. "There are sacred places all around us," he said. "They can be found in all of the Seven Directions. They are found in the East and in the North, in the South and in the West, as well as Above, Below, and the place Within. Without those places we lose our balance."

"Are Delawares the only Indian people with sacred places?"

Uncle Old Bear smiled. "No, Little Turtle. Everyone has sacred places. Later today, at the powwow, we will see Native people from all over this continent. Let me tell you about some of their special places."

Old Bear placed his hand again on the Earth and drew a cross in the circle. "We'll begin," he said, touching one of the arms of the cross, "just as the sun starts every day. We'll begin in the East."

I ONCE KNEW A MAN
who came from the land
where the light of dawn
first touches the shore.
Long ago, he said,
a giant lived with his people.
A friend to them,
that giant's name was Mau-shop.

Mau-shop brought them wood
and caught food for them,
cared for them as if
they were his children.
But the people forgot.
They were not thankful.
Then one day the Creator
spoke to Mau-shop, saying,
"You have done enough.
Now the people must learn
to take care of themselves."

Mau-shop saw that his work
of helping the people was done.
He turned himself into a whale,
a great white whale that swam off to the East,
beyond the cliffs glowing bright
with the light of the dawn,
which shows us the strength
brought by every day.

EAST

Wampanoag

To THE NORTH
live the Longhouse People,
near the edge of the falls called Ne-ah-ga.

They sometimes spoke of the Thunder Beings
who lived in a cave beneath the falls.
When a child wanted to give thanks
to the Thunderers for the gift of rain,
he would place an offering in a canoe
and put it in the river to float over the falls.

One day a young woman,
alone in her canoe,
was crossing the river
far up from the falls
when she lost her paddle.
The current was swift and
she found herself swept away.
This brave young woman
had always been a friend of the Thunderers,
giving them gifts with each new season.
So, as she fell, she did not scream or cry.
In trust, she asked calmly for help.

The Thunder Beings
saved her life,
catching her safely in their blanket.
Then the chief of the Thunderers
asked that young woman to be his wife.
She agreed, and to this day,
the Seneca say that when the rumbling voices
of the Thunder Beings roll across the sky,
the brave young woman is keeping watch,
reminding us that every gift we give
gives us back a blessing.

NORTH

Seneca

*F*ROM A FRIEND
who lives in the land of mesas
I heard the story of how, long ago,
life was hard because there were many monsters.
One of the worst was called
He-Who-Kicks-Them-Over-the-Cliff—
an ogre who waited on the mountain trail.
Though many tried, no one could defeat him.

There were two brothers, the Hero Twins.
They decided to go out and fight all the monsters.
Grandmother Spider said she would help them.
She quietly crept up to the place where
He-Who-Kicks-Them-Over-the-Cliff was sleeping.
Then she wove her web over his eyes.

When the Hero Twins came,
they pushed the ogre over that cliff.
When he struck the Earth, he became a great stone.
Although some people call it El Capitan,
the Navajo know that it once was that monster.
It stands there to this day, a sacred symbol
of how good can overcome evil.

WEST

Navajo

*I*F WE SHOULD TRAVEL
far to the South,
there in the land
of mountains and mist,
we might hear the story
of how Earth was first shaped.

Water Beetle came out
to see if it was ready,
but the ground was
still as wet as a swamp,
too soft for anyone to stand.

Great Buzzard said, "I will help dry the land."
He began to fly close above the new Earth.
Where his wings came down,
valleys were formed,
and where his wings lifted,
hills rose up through the mist.

So the many rolling valleys and hills
of that place called the Great Smokies
came into being there.
And so it is that the Cherokee people,
aware of how this land was given,
know that the Earth is a sacred gift
we all must respect and share.

SOUTH

Cherokee

$\mathcal{F}$AR FROM HERE
to the West is a desert land where
I'itoi, the Elder Brother,
looked out and then said to the people,
"In this place you will live
as long as you remember
all around you is sacred."

Though it seems to be empty and dry,
the desert is always filled with life.
Those tall cactuses that lift their arms
up into the sky are ancient people
who promised to always look over those
chosen to live in this sandy place.
The clouds in the sky are also alive.
They are ancient beings who care for the people.
They will answer with rain
when you ask for their help.

Here in the desert, where the air is clear,
you can hear the sound of
blessing rains, which come
after the people pray,
asking the clouds once more
to bring the sacred moisture
singing from their rainhouse
on the eastern horizon.
Then, as the ocotillo turns green
and the saguaro cactuses blossom,
they watch the cycle of life begin again.

WEST

Papago

*T*HERE ARE ALSO SOME PLACES
where our stories
were shaped in the Earth
by people long gone.

South of the great freshwater sea,
in the place called O-hi-yo,
there is such a hill.

There, a great Earth serpent,
like the spirit of water,
which gives life to our crops,
circles a hilltop, shaped out of Earth.
Carried in baskets, it was made
by the people who understood
its meaning two thousand years ago.

It is so long that when you stand
at one end of it,
you cannot see the other.

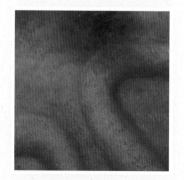

All that we know now
about that sacred place
is that the people
once went there to pray.
It helps us remember
all of this Earth is alive.

CENTER
Hopewell

*I*N THE PLACE

where great mountains rise up to the sky,
Buffalo went to the humans and said,
"From now on, you will be our slaves."
"That is not right," the humans replied.
"Our Creator meant all to respect one another."

"We will prove we are strongest,"
Buffalo said. "Let us have a race.
The one who wins will hunt the other."
So it was that they would race
from the Black Hills to the Rocky Mountains.
With Buffalo were Deer, Antelope, and Elk.
Dog, Eagle, and Falcon chose to help the humans.

The race began, and Deer ran so fast that
when Man reached Dog he was far behind.
Antelope drew further ahead,
but Elk and Eagle, as they raced each other,
reached Buffalo and Falcon at the same time.
Falcon circled up into the sky, and then,
just as it seemed Buffalo would win,
Falcon dove down to the top of the mountain.

Since that day, to honor Falcon and Eagle,
the people wear their sacred feathers.
The faithful Dog shares with the people
their homes and their food.
When the people hunt Buffalo
they do so with that same respect
the Creator wished for all beings.

ABOVE

Cheyenne

A HOPI FRIEND
once told me that the people came
from another world beneath this world.
Before that world,
they lived in another and
another one still, so that the world
we live in today is the fourth one
the people have known.

Each time, it seems,
things were going well,
until something happened
that made things go wrong.
People acted jealous,
people fought one another.
People didn't remember to respect the sacred.
Coyote caused the greatest trouble,
when he stole the child of the water monster.
When the water monster took back its child,
the whole third world was washed over by flood.

So the people left their old world behind.
They had to climb higher
to another, safer place.

Perhaps that great canyon
in the heart of their lands
was meant to remind us
of those worlds that were lost
before we reached this rainbow world
no one wants to leave behind.

BELOW
Hopi

NO ONE LIVES TODAY
in the ancient houses built by
the old people high up in the cliffs.
People lived well then, safe from enemies,
while growing their corn and beans and squash
in gardens watered by the ditches they made.

But they say one man grew too proud back then.
He thought all the people should work for him.
Though he was a leader, he forgot that those
who lead should always think first of the people.

For a while the people did as he said,
hoping one day his heart would grow kind.
Instead, he grew crueler every day,
until at last the people could stand it no longer.

Their leader had lost the sacred balance,
and so they would no longer serve him.
They all left that city high on the cliff
and went to a place where the people's lives
were again as free as the flow of water.

Now only the wind sings through the ruins
of a place whose broken stones remind us
that real power can only be held
by those whose hands are open.

BALANCE LOST
Walapai

A LONG LINE
of islands rests in the big lake our Abenaki cousins
called Pe-ton-bowk, the waters in between.
Those islands are stones
dropped from the hands of Od-zi-ho-zo,
the ancient one who shaped this lake
when he rose from the land.

Thunder Beings lived on each of those islands,
frightening the people with their shouts.

Then a hero named Be-deg-wad-zo
went to them one after another,
asking them to live up in the sky
because their great voices
had such sacred strength they
made all the people afraid.

Be-deg-wad-zo said to the people then,
"Always show respect
when you are on the lake,
for those islands are places
still owned by the thunder."

Sometimes that which is filled with power
is best known from a distance—
not forgotten, but given respect.

BALANCE HELD
Abenaki

OLD BEAR and Little Turtle stood together on the hill.

"My uncle," he said, "I see now what you mean. Every place we go is a sacred place if we remember that we always carry the teachings with us."

Old Bear nodded as he placed his hand on his chest. "Little Turtle," he said, "you understand. Here is where we must look to see the sacred places that are all around us. We must look within, through the eyes of our hearts. Everything is sacred between Earth and Sky."

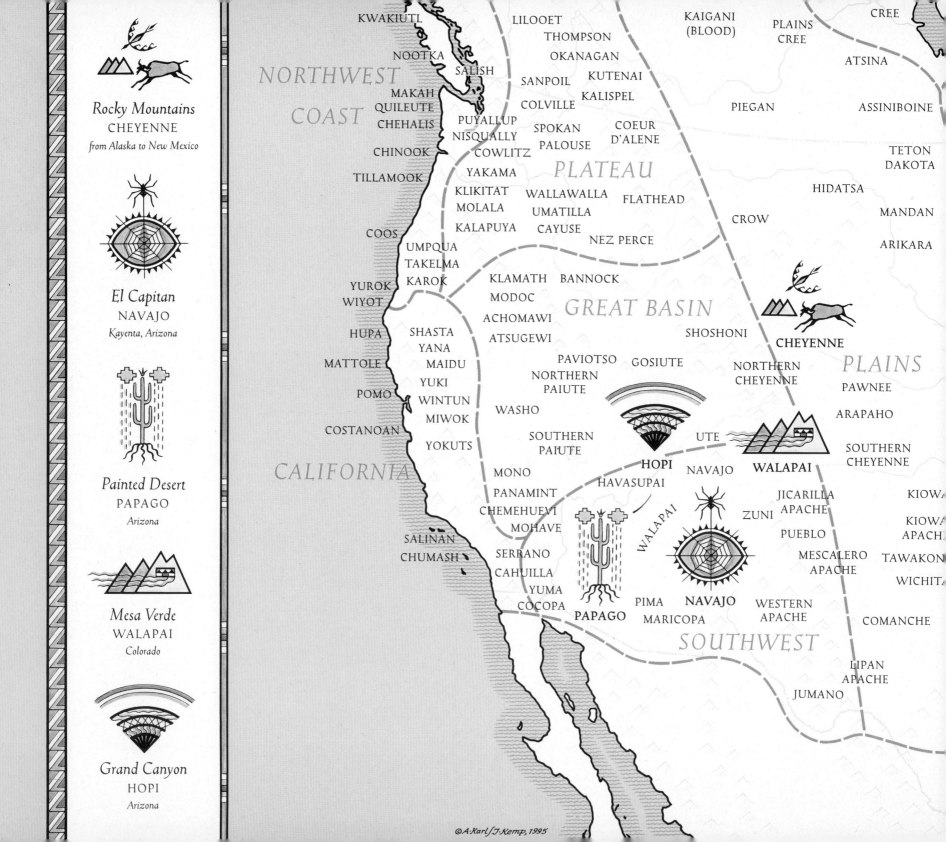

CREE

SUBARCTIC

OJIBWA
(CHIPPEWA)

OTTAWA

SENECA

TIONONTATI

NEUTRAL

SENECA

MICMAC
MALECITE
PASSAMAQUODDY

HURON

ABENAKI

PENOBSCOT

PENNACOOK

ABENAKI

WAMPANOAG

MAHICAN

MOHAWK
ONEIDA
ONONDAGA
CAYUGA

NIPMUC

MASSACHUSET
NAUSET   NIANTIC
NARRAGANSETT
PEQUOT
MOHEGAN
WAPPINGER

SANTEE
DAKOTA

YANKTON
DAKOTA

PONCA   IOWA

MISSOURI

OMAHA

OTO

KANSA

OSAGE

MENOMINEE

WINNEBAGO

MESQUAKI

KICKAPOO

KASKASKIA

PEORIA

PLANKASHAW

POTAWATOMI

MIAMI

HOPEWELL

SUSQUEHANNA
(CONESTOGA)

PAMUNKEY

POWHATAN

CHICKAHOMINY

MATTAPONY

TUTELO

NOTTAWAY

TUSCARORA

CATAWBA

DELAWARE (LENNI LENAPE)
NANTICOKE

PAMLICO

ILLINOIS

EASTERN WOODLAND

SHAWNEE

CHEROKEE

QUAPAW

CHICKASAW

SOUTHEAST

CADDO

CHOCTAW

KICHAI   TUNICA

WACO

TONKAWA

NATCHEZ

HOUMA

ATAKAPA

CHITIMACHA

BILOXI

MOBILE

ALABAMA

APALACHEE

YUCHI

TUSKEGEE

CREEK

HITCHITI

YAMASEE

GUALE

TIMUCUA

SEMINOLE

CALUSA

Native North America has always been a world of many peoples. The map on the preceding spread shows the locations of many of those original Native nations, most of which still exist to this day.

Because BETWEEN EARTH & SKY draws from so many different tribes and regions to tell its stories, here, as a guide, are some suggested pronunciations to the words of those peoples.

Abenaki	ab-eh-na´-kē
Be-deg-wad-zo	peh-tay-kwah-dzō
Cherokee	cher-ə-kē
Cheyenne	shī-an
El Capitan	el kap´-i-tan´
Hopewell	hōp´-wel
Hopi	hō-pē
I'itoi	i´-i-tō-ē
Kit-se-le-mu-kong	kit´-se-le-mu´-kong
Ma-hi-ka-ni-tewk	mah-hē-kah´-nē-took
Mau-shop	mow-shop
Navajo	nav´-ə-hō
Ne-ah-ga	ney-ah´-gah
Od-zi-ho-zo	ods´-ē-hō-sō
O-hi-yo	o-hē´-yoh
Papago	pä-pə-gō
Pe-ton-bowk	pā-tōn´-bowk
Seneca	sen´-ə-kə
Walapai	wah-lah-pī
Wampanoag	wam-pah-nō-əg´